Restless

Published by Nordisk Books, 2020
www.nordiskbooks.com

Kenneth Moe, 2015. First published by Pelikanen.
Acquired through Immaterial Agents.

This translation has been published with the financial
support of NORLA

Cover design © Nordisk Books
Printed and bound in Great Britain by Clays Ltd,
Elcograf S.p.A.

A CIP catalogue record for this book is
available from the British Library
ISBN 9780995485273

Kenneth Moe
Restless

Translated by
Alison McCullough

nordisk books

Also by Nordisk Books

Havoc
Tom Kristensen

*You can't betray your best friend
and learn to sing at the same time*
Kim Hiorthøy

Love/War
Ebba Witt-Brattström

Zero
Gine Cornelia Pedersen

Termin
Henrik Nor-Hansen

Transfer Window
Maria Gerhardt

Inlands
Elin Willows

'The amorous subject cannot write his love story himself.'

Roland Barthes,
A Lover's Discourse: Fragments

You ask whether I'm writing about you and the short answer is 'yes' and the rest of this fumbling letter can be the long one. You'd like to hear everything, I'm sure, conceited as you are: how I fell in love with you, how I still long for you – and then you'll probably want me to find poetry in all this misery, and to pull some wisdom out of my ass, and admittedly I should be able to manage that.

Lonely people know something about life too! …

That last sentence has been grinding around in my head for a good while now, but I don't trust it, just as I'm sceptical of most of what I think and for fleeting moments try to believe in. Because what do I really know? Nothing. I know nothing. I can hardly be said to be living, precisely because I *don't* know, because I need to know *before* I can live – while life is arranged such that one only knows anything after the fact. As a child I read a book about reincarnation. It said that in each life, one must learn something new. I remember thinking that in this one I'd learn patience.

How much can one really learn about life through the cracks in the blinds?

I've started to realise that such days can make up a whole life: an entire life filled with longing and nothing else. I have to do something, and so I write letters. I can tell you about New Year's Eve, for example – that at first I was served glass after glass of wine and had a good time, but when the fireworks lit up the sky above the park and I knew that everything was exactly as before, and that my life wasn't likely to undergo any noteworthy changes this year, either, it was as if everything inside me turned dark, and on my way home in the early hours of the first day of the first month I repeatedly punched my fist into a brick wall until several of my knuckles were bleeding. I understand I have no right to be angry. But on the other hand it would be dishonest to censor the idiot in me, or to pretend to be a stronger person than I actually am. The whole point is that I don't want to lie anymore, or to 'play my cards right.'

When you struggle, as I did, to impress another person, and manage only to satisfy that person's silly neuroses, you start to wonder what she's worth, what you yourself are worth – what the rest of it's worth. My longing and your vanity must have been inextricably linked from the start: the fact that I want to look at you, that you want to be looked at. A skewed starting point, to put it mildly.

You're probably hoping that this will be a tender, heartfelt letter, something funny you can tell everyone about: the poor hopeless bastard who fell for you and so wrote you a hundred pages. That it'll be almost like a romance novel, with you as the main character.

Perhaps you played the muse, fickle and enchanting, precisely so that I would write you such a letter. Perhaps your own poetry was nothing but pretence. Perhaps you've never really wanted to write, but rather to *become* poetry…Insulted yet?

I promise to give you the literary treatment you deserve.

What is a person worth *alone*, outside the contexts where values arise and attain their legitimacy?

Nothing.

Lonely people know nothing and are worth nothing.

My room is as empty as the rest of my life. I find it stressful to be surrounded by things. I have hardly any books anymore, and barely any furniture: a small table, a box mattress for a bed, an armchair, a stool for my feet. The walls used to be empty, too, but I've put up some quotations, a couple of Rodin sketches of naked ballerinas touching themselves, a postcard S– once sent me from Berlin – a picture of Travis Bickle with a revolver – and a photo of an old Afghan hag with a Kalashnikov rifle clamped between her legs. The air in here is cold, but that's the kind of thing that probably makes one stronger. If the windows aren't left mostly open the room starts to take on the smell of the sour towels in the dirty laundry basket, the rankness of my sweat and the stale sweetness of semen from the wastepaper basket. I spend way too much of my time here and can breathe the stagnant air for hours before I start to notice it.

We talk all the time in the dark. I give good explanations for everything, persuading you day by day. You're not really here, and so can never really leave me, either. At night you snuggle up to me in bed: your slim body with its small breasts against mine. I think even your body is humble. It doesn't make much of itself. You leaf through the pages of the books – tell me I read such strange ones. You tease me. I read Marcus Aurelius in bed. I read La Rochefoucauld. He writes: 'Weak people cannot be sincere.' I read the sentence aloud to you.

There are some glasses on the table and a stack of four or five dirty plates. On them are congealed yellow globs of egg and red blobs of ketchup. I used to be someone who kept things in order, made sure to keep my surroundings clean and tidy, but I no longer have the energy for stuff like that. Lately, when I think about how I used to be this way or that, I often realise that it's been many years since I used to be that kind of person, or since I did things in this way or the other. Perhaps I was *never* like that. Maybe *this* is me. Maybe the dirty plates, the greasy stains left on the glasses by my hands and lips, are me?

I've always struggled to distinguish between self-loathing and self-awareness.

I don't even like my own name. If I'd been a girl, then according to my mother I would have been called Kari – which incidentally was also the name of my first girlfriend. It was my older brother who suggested the name that I ended up with; it had been the name of a good friend he'd had to leave behind when our family moved. The name is among the most common to appear in crime and bankruptcy statistics. There are nineteen Norwegians with the same combination of first and last name as me. The most well-known of them is in prison for dealing a record amount of drugs.

These days, whenever I think *your* name, it's like the blaring of an alarm clock in the morning after a sleepless night.

I myself have never committed any serious misdeed, but I feel a kind of kinship with the scum of the earth, with the rapists and mass murderers – as if they could tell me something about myself, as if they were the caricature that brought out the truth about me. Those of us with an overactive conscience so easily identify with those who have no conscience at all. Perhaps we long to commit real crimes, skin and all, and to be punished for them. Maybe we long for a cell that is, after all, larger than that of our own thoughts; an existence with solid walls and a defined timeframe. And maybe we suspect that a world without crime would be an even greater hell on earth, because then nobody would be aware that all these terrible things we go around thinking about exist.

On my way home from a night on the town late one evening in winter, I was passing a takeout place when someone called out: *Don't give him pizza, he's a rapist! Don't! He's a rapist! Don't give him pizza!* ... and although the man wasn't speaking about me – even though I've never raped anyone or even wanted to, and it therefore *couldn't* be me he was talking about – I immediately identified with the pizza customer, as if my depraved thoughts were on a scale equal to his alleged acts.

First it was the eyes... I should say: of course. And what was it about yours, exactly? I once tried to compliment Kari on hers. She said, almost rolling them: 'It's not the eyes themselves, but what's around them, that makes one pair different from another!' And around your pair of blues, what? Big, blushing cheeks. The tip of a nose that's pulled up and down by your upper lip when you talk. Small, dark brows that are likewise never still. Constant movement in every muscle. A face completely free of secrets. My first impression was that you radiated something nervously innocuous I did not trust. I had to find something ugly, fast. Had to protect myself. Had to reject you before you had the chance to reject me. You looked at me, sort of seductively over your glass of beer, though I didn't draw that conclusion then – but I did decide that your gaze was faithless, faithless and searching, and that you were the kind of person one falls for against one's will. Resolved, I pointed at your eyes and said: 'Those things won't work on me.'

A useless state: I mainly lie in bed, thinking about you, or sit here in my armchair, or stand by the window and spy on what's going on outside. But I might at least be able to write a few paragraphs about what it's like just to lie or to sit or to stand here; what it's like to do nothing but think of you. Every time I think I'm getting a handle on the story it changes into something else. It cracks, breaking up into small pieces. It doesn't shatter, but rather cracks like safety glass... each piece remaining stuck in a kind of fractured whole. I have hundreds of beginnings and that's really all I have, written down here and there, now and then, without any kind of plan. Just a mass of passing moments I'm unable to get out of my head. I should make it clear, before I forget, that I'm not writing just to propagate my own misery, but so that something might fall into place. *Something...* Some kind of practical truth. I have only one book in me at the end of the day: it's titled *How I Learned to Love*, and I hope to write it over and over again, with small variations, until I die.

Imagine that I were capable of stalking you on the street, of throwing stones at your window at night; of shoving threats and the hearts of animals, psychotic mix tapes and home-knit scarves through your letterbox; of killing and ending up in prison for you – because what else constitutes trying hard enough? Is it ever time to give up on love? And what is love worth if I'm able to stay composed? If all it awakens in me is thought after thought? What fails to lead to action is worthless… and if this should lead to action, of what kind? Because every now and then I think of something idiotic I've said to you and want to put an end to myself to be spared having to remember it – or more simply, to put an end to you to rid myself of the witness. I'm sure you know what a coward I really am, but all these things exist inside me and want to get out of me, and so must be made into *something*.

Every day during spring, women sprint up the stairs in the narrow passageway between the buildings. I can see them, but they can't see me. When the shade falls across the window and my room is completely dark, I sometimes stand naked at its centre and follow them with my gaze. They run up, pause for a moment, wipe the sweat off their brows, walk slowly back down and then run up again. In running tights. In dripping-wet tops with sports bras underneath. With practical ponytails or braids, and music in their ears. Or, like now, with my back to them, I hear only the sound of their steps – *tp-tp-tp-tp-tp-tp* – up the stairs. 'I'll be ready for them soon,' I find myself thinking. 'I'll be ready soon.' Women running up and down outside the window, trees that will soon turn green – I'm actually quite lucky. More and more often, I think: my life is pretty good. Or rather, the thought pops up of its own accord, only to immediately rub up against certain realities.

I've not earned a single penny over the past six months. Last year, during summer, I replaced the timber cladding on a house. Some of the boards were so rotten you could squeeze sap from them after a heavy downpour. It should've been almost miraculous – fixing a house with one's own hands! … I'd hoped it'd prove something, teach me something about life, build character, or *something*, but all I got was pain in my right shoulder. In the end I could hardly lift my arm. For a while it simply hung there, like a koala clung to my side. Now I'm living on a student loan for a course I've already quit. All I want is this. Only this.

Beautiful sentences are a kind of protest against what I know – deep down – is the truth about myself.

When literature gets in the way of life, and life in the way of literature, they must be brought together in new ways.

My mother recently told me that when I was a child, I used to chew holes in all my t-shirts. 'Look,' I said, pointing at the holes in the t-shirt I was wearing. I still like to chew them when I'm worried or can't concentrate. Most of my trousers hang off me now (I'm eating less and less). The other day I put a big rip in my favourite pair, the old ones that almost fit me again. The other pair I like are missing a button. Both pairs of jogging bottoms I own are missing their drawstrings. My trainers are falling apart. In one of my black pairs of boxer shorts I found an orange stain. At first I thought it was organic, that the neon colour had dripped out of me, but on closer inspection it turned out to be embedded in the fabric itself.

Today the sun is shining on my street again, but I have my back to the light and the trees outside the window. I've always been the type to shut myself in my room for days, weeks at a time, to work on some project or other that I think will save me, without any clear idea as to exactly why this one should save me when none of my previous projects have. Right now, for example: a book, a letter. I've chosen this solitude because I prefer it, but I've never chosen to prefer solitude, and would have preferred to prefer something else. All my longings are equally paradoxical. I constantly doubt whether I *should* want you and what I'd use you for should I get you, but I know that…

Through the café window I saw you take a drag of your boyfriend's cigarette and then kiss him. He's much taller than you – you had to stand on tiptoe and crane your neck to reach his lips. Why you, I thought – why did I have to get so wrapped up in you? You're just like everyone else. A pair of eyes, a pair of thighs, with desire between them and an impenetrable mind full of provisional convictions. I've tried to understand, but always come back to the same zen-like conclusion: there's nothing to understand. There is no 'M–'. She who stood there with her boyfriend that evening was nothing but body and words – as was he who sat and watched them. The clearer my thinking, the more I see through both you and myself, the worse it feels. The passion persists, but has been shown to be worthless; just an empty chest I drag around with me.

It's morning and I'm happy, because I lift up the blinds and see blue. Every year I fall victim to the springtime fallacy: I interpret the longer days, the sound of lawnmowers, the smell of freshly mown grass and so on as a sign that life is about to become irrevocably better. There's a man on the steps outside the window; he lifts a crow from the step he's standing on and sets it on the branch of a tree. He stares up at the bird in astonishment as it flies away, as if it should (as if it could) have done anything else.

It's night-time and I'm unhappy. In the dark, a mayfly and a tiny moth are fighting for my attention in front of the laptop screen. It glows too brightly. I turn the brightness down only to turn it back up again – I'm never satisfied. My eyes will soon be shot to hell. I should be writing. I'm not waiting for inspiration, but to get rid of the inspiration I already have. On some level, maybe all books are an attempt to break the connection between the work and the obsession that inspires the work, so that for the briefest of moments one is free to let new obsessions grow.

I observe you, I take notes, I look for patterns and correlations, formulate hypotheses and imagine breakthroughs, but all of it's just *bullshit*, because I want you to be complicated so that I can *think* all the time, instead of accepting the obvious – that you simply don't want me, and that your sudden indifference today and this grief I'm feeling is as random as all other bodily sensations arising and passing away. The coldness of my room this evening. The warmth beneath the blanket. My runny nose. Nothing but allergens between us at the end of the day; meaningless reactions to reactions. Nothing but your scatter-brained desire and my stupid feelings; nothing but objects colliding in infinite space.

The outline of a phantom door bulges beneath the wallpaper. A large, upright rectangle is all that remains of the opening that used to exist between my room and the neighbouring one, before I moved in. It's been closed with plasterboard, or something. There's nothing but circumstantial evidence that I live with other people: a crusted lump of toothpaste in the wash basin in the bathroom. Dark, curly hairs in the drain beneath the shower. Crumbs on the kitchen worktop. The good knife already dirty and in the dishwasher whenever I need it. We're like poltergeists to each other in this apartment. Whenever I hear a sound in the hall, by the time I go out to investigate the presence has already vanished.

One woman of flesh and blood has been in here with me so far this year. 'Do you want to fuck me?' she asked. I lay half on top of her on the bed and stroked the outside of her lips until she was wet enough for my entire thumb. She started to take off her clothes, then mine. I didn't really want to. At first my penis simply hung there, like a slug. 'Take all the time you need,' she said. It was half-hard and terror-stricken when I eventually managed to push it in. When at last we were finished, she asked whether it was okay if she smoked. 'Not really,' I said. 'Out of the window, I suppose.' She sat in the armchair, naked apart from the t-shirt I'd lent her, and lit a cigarette. 'You seemed miles away,' she said. She came, but I didn't – not until she finished me off with her mouth. I'd tried to forget, but had forgotten nothing. She told me she'd soon be admitted. 'Voluntarily!' she added quickly, and giggled. Over the following days I found long, blonde hairs everywhere. In the hairbrush she'd borrowed. Among my bedlinen and clothes.

I'd so like to have suffered proper heartbreak – to have cried some, fucked a load of idiots and then been done with it, because that's what you do, you fuck your way through to the other side, as if one hole were as good as any other, as if they had anything to do with each other, as if there were some kind of mystical connection between cunts and they were all sources of the same esoteric wisdom, or portals to some parallel universe where love were more concrete than concrete… I can just imagine it: all women and all men, everyone except me, united in endless, incomprehensible, cosmic-vaginal contractions. Only *I* stand here, outside – old-fashioned, romantic, fixated, weak.

'It's going to rain,' you said. 'It's not going to rain,' I said. The dark clouds gathered above us and soon covered the entire sky. We lay there on the blanket. Thunder. Lightning. I grabbed your arm and stretched my own arm up towards the lightning bolts to scare you. You gasped with laughter and fear like a child. You tried to pull your arm back, but I held on tight. Then the rain fell over us and the lake. I'll never forget your face then, un-made-up, the rainwater in your hair. I want you to imagine that all of this was written that night in the rain. Imagine the letters dripping from the strands of our hair down onto the paper. That the ink simply fell that way because it had to. 'I didn't think I could,' I said, 'before I fell in love with you.' 'I'm attracted to you,' you said, 'In a weird way. I'd enjoy fucking you – but it's not worth losing my boyfriend over.'

I wake at dawn as usual. The neighbour above me always puts his mobile phone on the floor and it vibrates at seven o'clock each morning. Then he keeps me awake through all his morning routines, with his awful stomping back and forth. With every step he takes, the lamp between my bed and chair clinks in its protective glass, slightly loose around the bulb. The sound of his feet penetrates right through my ears and into the primitive part of the brain on the lookout for predators. I put music on, but can still hear him through my headphones. I turn the music up to the maximum volume, but can still feel the shaking. Only after he's jogged down the stairs (which, by the way, go right past the wall my bed is pushed up against) and has slammed the front door at around eight o'clock do I manage to get back to sleep again. Then I sleep for as long as I can. I've been a morning person lately anyway. It changes from week to week, the kind of person I am.

This is how the days move: I sleep later, wake even later, sleep even later, and so on, until I've cycled all the way through and have a relatively normal rhythm for a few days, before the process starts all over again. Lately I've been out of breath upon waking – that can't be a good sign. The other day I had a dream where I laughed and laughed, but when I woke, it sounded just like crying. Maybe that's why I'm exhausted when I wake up? Perhaps every awakening is a transition from laughter to tears? Today I woke up lying on a fold in the sheet and was momentarily convinced it was a tumour in my stomach. Spring winds bring the smell of burnt cocoa all the way here from the chocolate factory. I recognise it from when I lived close by, breathing it in every day. It's suffocating. Some days, the greatest distance in the universe is the metre from the edge of the bed to my trousers, which lie in a heap on the floor, and this is one of those days. I stay in bed as the sun comes up; am still there when it disappears again. Finally, I sit down in the chair.

My ass sinks deeper and deeper into the armchair. It used to belong to my father, and over time has become quite worn out. Now it's my office: I sit and write in it, and live most of my life here. The chair has gradually adapted itself to the shape of my body. Every day, I sink a little deeper into it. Every day it becomes more comfortable, more and more an adequate substitute for actually doing something with my life. I purge nothing by sitting here and fiddling about with words, discovering only more ambiguities to investigate, and ambiguities within the ambiguities. Turns out I'm sitting on a peanut. Foam rubber started falling out of the bottom of the chair the other day. I had to pick up some bits that had come loose and wind steel wire around them to hold the underside in place. Then it became possible to zip it shut, and thus I solved the problem of the foam rubber. This is how I keep busy, solving small problems, while the big ones get bigger.

I'm full of solutions, but the solutions aren't interesting in the way that the problem is interesting, because the solutions aren't *me*, in the way that the problem is.

I'm no longer looking to seduce with my words, as you've probably noticed, but simply to move on, just to grow up, dammit... but I keep constantly getting stuck on all kinds of stuff; cactuses, thistles, longings, humiliations... The trick is to write ever shorter paragraphs, so that I don't get caught up in details from the past: your lyrical accent, for instance, and the high-pitched music of your voice; how the sound of you softens up a room, how your femininity seems to float on its—

Damn! ...

I just want to leap from stone to stone without falling into the water.

I just want to—

43

I don't want to leap from stone to stone in order to avoid strong feelings, but precisely to get close to them, without getting pulled under by them. So let's say I step on a wet stone, okay. My foot slips and gets wet up to the heel. I feel the ice-cold river, the goosebumps breaking out across my skin (*that something is lived!*) – but I don't fall face first into the water, don't flounder. I quickly get up and keep going.

N– is wondering what I'm living on, seeing as I gave up my rhetoric studies several months ago and still haven't found a job. I say that I'm as yet still receiving my student loan. 'But…' She doesn't understand. 'Isn't that a *shame*?' A strong word, *shame* – but she was born and raised in Colombia, and I conclude that they must have different values there, more conservative perhaps. I smile at her honesty – appreciate it, actually. 'Yes,' I say, 'perhaps it is shameful. But right now it's just so important for me to keep writing.' She's only recently learned the language and understands from my reaction that she's made a mistake. She's confused the Norwegian word 'skam' (shame) with the English 'scam'. 'Isn't that a scam?' is what she meant to ask, not 'Isn't that shameful?' We laugh at the misunderstanding. But it's true, I think, regardless: I'm an ashamed and shameful scam artist, without a job, without money, who just sits on his ass and thinks, feels, writes at the government's expense – as if the anthill that is Norway has use for a single, chosen ant that does nothing but polish his own feelers.

I don't want to struggle any more, or try to impress. I simply want the words to crawl under your skin, beneath your beautiful surface – to where you're just as ugly as everyone else – and lay their eggs there. I want to try to present myself as I really am in this letter, with all my impure intentions and loose skin and eighteen extra kilos on my body. Every time I walk past the mirror I lift my t-shirt to study my stomach. Flabby. Hairy. The more pounds I lose, the more the stretched skin hangs over my belt, like a sweaty balloon blown all the way up and then emptied of air again. Desperation is all that remains now, and perhaps there's something beautiful about it, something that might awaken a *new* desire in you. One creates nothing with common sense, but must be desperate every single day on earth. Isn't integrity simply saying and doing a whole bunch of stupid things with one's head held high? And isn't integrity more attractive than the suffocating resignation and common sense that's all around us?

When my heart beats faster I start to get suspicious. I try to interpret the rhythm. My pulse seems to know something it isn't telling me. A— says that I treat my feelings like a foreign body, and maybe I do, but how else is one supposed to figure them out? I'm not in the habit of listening to my immediate sensations, those that try to pull me every which way, first this way and then that. I've always been most intimate with *words* — that is, with the faculty that's usually (and rather naively) called 'reason', but which is often just pure sanitation of instinct, of necessary pain. I often think I'm too practically inclined to hurt in a way that feels real.

By the way: was it experience or the words themselves that convinced me of their power?

It's the curse of the doubter that everything must first be tied to words in order to be real, and then those words should be linked to other words, which should preferably add up to something greater, as in a math problem. Only when one has a good, coherent description of the things in the world is one ready to act in it.

Precision is my pathology. I am a pedant of the emotions.

I'm well aware that I can't trust these thoughts born of grief. I have a certain distance from them, a knack for irony. And writing – this great effort to get these bitter thoughts down on paper – what is it if not a prayer for everything to be ironic from beginning to end? The first thing one learns from language is that it can't be taken seriously, and so one should talk about misery as much as possible in order to expose it as a joke, a play on words. Only rarely should one talk of happiness and energy. Isn't this the function of literature, perhaps: not to exalt pain, but to describe it to death, and then feed the bitterness back into the bloodstream, like a stoic vaccine?

A book is an attempt to become a better person – or else it is nothing.

I watch episode after episode of Carl Sagan's *Cosmos* until I fall asleep in the chair and wake here in the middle of the night. The last I remember of my dreams is that I was floating above a pair of naked thighs. They stretched out like an endless valley on an alien planet, and I: a space traveller. The episodes have kept playing as I slept with my computer in my lap. When I wake, Carl is back on earth and talking about the library in Alexandria. When he says that the library contained a million scrolls at the time of its destruction, I almost cry. 'It's gone,' he says, 'utterly and forever.'

In my half dreams before I fall fully asleep it feels as if I'm walking around an abandoned stage set, as if my brain hasn't yet managed to fill it. I walk through isolated film sets alone, looking for something unknown, perhaps something proper to dream about: people, bodies. You almost never appear in my dreams. I don't know why, that's just how it is. Last night, as I slept, I remembered something seemingly arbitrary from winter: a pram that would soon be loaded down with snow, and a baby inside it, wrapped up snugly. The child squirmed and cried inside its white blanket, reminiscent of a huge larva. It felt as if I thought about the larva for hours – but it probably only lasted a few minutes or seconds.

My mysterious allergy has flared up again. I try eye drops, try antihistamines. I vacuum and vacuum, stay away from cats and all other kinds of animals, close the windows for days, weeks at a time. I scratch myself until I almost bleed – at least the tears which seep from my eyes, after I've poked around in them with a finger, smell like blood. Is it perhaps *your* fault that my eyes are running, that my throat is burning, that I sneeze every other minute and that my nose occasionally starts to bleed? And if so, do you not have a responsibility to make me well again, if loneliness is the cause?

Maybe it has something to do with the mould that's growing just behind my pillow. I'm breathing it in at night, devouring millions of spores as I sleep deeply and innocently, dreaming strange dreams. I wash away the mould with bleach when it appears, but it only comes back stronger; smells fresh, like trees, and just as damp. It seems to whisper to me when I'm half asleep, communicating with something inside me, something rotten in my marrow. Some bloodied crookedness. It's the spores it speaks to, the spores I've inhaled – her children. The spores have taken root in my spine, spread to my brain and taken over, making me make the same mistakes over and over again, like a liver fluke-infected ant.

I waited outside the bathroom as you brushed your teeth. It was after some party. When you came out, I asked whether you'd like to come into the bedroom with me. 'I'm not sure that's such a good idea,' you said. 'It doesn't mean anything,' I said, placing my hand on your back. You walked into the room ahead of me without saying anything further. Here's how it played out: you fell asleep in my arms almost at once, lay there smacking your lips, and I lay there feeling your breath mixed with wine and toothpaste against my face, felt how my penis beat my pulse against your thigh. Eventually I fell asleep too, waking only as you were sneaking out of the bed. You smiled at me in the light from the doorway before you disappeared.

Half a glass of lukewarm water on the table, bubbles of air at the top and all the way around it. Under the glass, an earlier draft of the manuscript, scribbled all over with arrows and idiosyncratic abbreviations. A pile of post-its and notes. The wrapper from a bar of chocolate containing 2.9g net carbs. Two opened envelopes. Electricity bill. Internet bill. Unpaid. A stack of five just-read library books (to be returned as soon as possible). The blinds are closed, the reading lamp dimmed. A calmness in my body. Fingers sticky. The waistband of my trousers pulled partway down my thighs. Some paper towel stuffed inside my boxers. An image of you open in my web browser. A porn clip in the window beside it, paused. In the picture you're smiling, holding a big marzipan pig, Christmas decorations in the background. Photographer: your boyfriend.

Should I have written this letter with dignity? Excluded the deepest pits? The times I measured heartbreak against the guilt I would feel had I strangled you, like some tempered, hedonistic equation? Should I have pretended there was no violence in me? What about the fantasies in which I don't always treat you like a Disney princess? Should I have skipped those, too? I go crazy imagining it. My tongue in your wet slit, for instance, and far, far up your ass. Didn't want anything to do with anyone's ass before you, but now I want to taste every taste, smell every single smell, one burning thigh against each cheek as I drink you and black out from the juices, forgetting about love, forgetting about you and me, dying happily with my tongue in some nameless pussy. The desire first comes to my throat, like a friendly suffocation. You stroke my hair. You grab hold of it, pull it, then tighten your grasp. You press my face into you. (In a moment of longing, when fantasising about you, feeling your body with all of mine: realising with a shudder that I'm lying here alone, that the whole thing is only happening inside my own isolated skull.)

I cannot touch this loneliness any more than I can touch the people around me, can only see from the calendar that even more time has passed without me being able to do anything about it. Everything simply flows, there's nobody here in relation to whom I can set limits. I can't become anything discrete. I'm an object without a subject, a subject without an object. A kind of metaphysical goo. Just me and my armchair here and soon we too will melt into each other. (Why does loneliness lead to self-investigation when the only way out is to investigate *others*? I'm burrowing deeper and deeper into myself. Lacking proper objects, I become my own.)

Every Saturday morning I fry pancakes for breakfast. This is what I have to look forward to all week, my sole predictable satisfaction. They're not special pancakes. I don't call them by a French name and they have nothing food-like or healthy in them. I simply take eggs, flour and milk, stir them together in a bowl, and fry thin pancakes from the batter, putting them in a heatproof dish as I go along. I fry a tall stack, pile them up, and ceremoniously carry the dish into my room where I eat the pancakes with sugar sprinkled on them. I like them as plain as possible, needing only the sugar to crunch between my teeth. Only that: the feeling of sugar crunching between my teeth. This is the *only* thing I know will make me happy every time, every week, every Saturday morning, regardless of whatever else is going on in my life.

It was late summer or early autumn and the sun had already gone, not so much as a strip of sunset on the horizon. There was rubbish scattered about after the barbecue, and empty beer cans and wine bottles. The others had gone up to the house to drink more or to sleep. Only you and I stayed behind, sitting down by the water. A silence had fallen between us, and eventually inside my head, too – the alcohol had calmed the flow of my thoughts, leaving a sort of light, bubbly feeling inside me, a kind of uncomfortable anticipation. I got up and walked over to the boat that lay at the water's edge. I called out to you, and you came over. It was cold. I hardly knew you. I tried to push the boat to set it out on the water and you helped me, but it wouldn't budge. I sat on the side of the boat, and you jumped up, too. Your weight made the boat rock slightly, and I stumbled. I grabbed your arm and dragged you down into the water with me. You floundered, splashing about, then came up from the water to stand there, dripping wet. You hit me, hard – first on the left cheek, then the right, then once again on the left, before you ran away from me.

The certainty that a blood vessel can burst at any moment, that blood might at any time spurt out and clot around the most delicate structures of my brain, so that I'm no longer the person I was just seconds before, is for me more than an abstract understanding. Three or four years before I was born, when he was around the same age as I am now, perhaps even a little younger, my dad suffered exactly this kind of haemorrhage. I think about it often, that it'll soon be my turn. He was at work when it happened, had colleagues around him who could help him, take him to the hospital straight away. I mainly sit here in my room, by myself.

The sounds outside the window are always so soothing compared to the noise in here, especially at night. Lone cars rush past, a fair distance from one another. Light footsteps on the stairs every now and then. A drunken conversation too far away for me to catch any of its meaning. Now and again someone sings, and that's totally fine. Right now: rain. Car tyres on water. A moment of serenity. It's getting late. Almost time to go to bed. Lie there and listen. Try to sleep. A sound drifts over from a completely different part of the building, far off, indistinct. I can't decide whether it's the sound of a woman passionately making love or a dog barking.

December. Freezing cold. You stopped and I stopped. Your coat was still open. Under your coat you wore a conservative sweater with lace on it. I traced the pattern with my finger, said: 'Virtuous.' You buttoned up your coat. I walked slowly towards you as you stepped backwards towards the wall, until you were standing with your back up against it. 'I want to,' you said, 'but it won't work.' 'You're absolutely right,' I said, mostly because I'd read in books that that's what you're supposed to say, and it bought me a few minutes, because you were surprised, smiled and said: 'Am I?' You cupped my cheek with your hand. 'It's as if you can see right into me.' A tear ran from my eye as you said this, which you either thoughtfully or thoughtlessly wiped away, or maybe you simply couldn't stand to see the tear hanging there, dangling from my chin like that. You suggested we make snow angels and I thought: 'Is she retarded?' A few days later you wrote to me: 'I'm probably not as virtuous as you think,' but I never really thought you were particularly virtuous.

Nothing is just one thing. An invitation isn't just an invitation. A rejection isn't just a rejection. A no isn't simply a no (even though we must pretend it is). When interpreting others' actions and utterances, one shouldn't look for *intention*, but *sanction*. Not: 'What does she want?' but 'What is she giving me permission to do?'

According to a family rumour, when my mother's father was a baby, his mother left him out in the snow. It wasn't my grandfather who told me the story; he died several years before I was born. But it's as if part of me can remember the snow, has inherited it, even though I've only received the story second-hand from my mum, who would never have left me out in the snow. If it is true, as I've recently read, that trauma can be inherited, then it's not so strange that this memory, which isn't really a memory, lives so intensely within me. The first thing my grandfather experienced was rejection, and this rejection settled permanently within his cells, will have epigenetic ripple effects throughout countless generations. I have frostbitten blood in my veins.

It's quiet right now. I must make the most of quiet moments...
I intended that as the start of one of these pieces, but
got no further. Instead I threw the pile of paper at the
wall so that the pages fluttered around. I want to start
over, or maybe do something completely different with
my life. The sheets of paper are strewn across the bed,
across the floor. I gather them up into a bag and take
the bag outside. The backyard is narrow and full of
shadows; there's been talk of rats. The smell of cooking
leaks from an open window. Sunday dinner. Potatoes
and gravy. Normality.

It isn't proper for adults to read, or have anything to do with books, except when sick in some way or other. But aren't we *always* sick in some way or other?

Some kind of cancer is moving inside me. I close my mouth to keep it trapped inside. It tends to manifest itself as an even, uncomfortable pressure against my large intestine, but can move quickly to my kidneys and pancreas without warning. Like a tiny squirrel, it clambers around in me, swinging from organ to organ, first here, then there, not knowing that it is slowly but surely killing its host. At its highest point it feels like swollen lymph nodes, but every now and again it hides in my testicles, the right one mainly (it was already gone by the time the doctor examined them). It's an advanced cancer, a cancer that's torn itself free of the body to become an autonomous organism.

I wake from not being able to breathe, throw myself out of bed, run to the bathroom, an intense pressure in my ribcage. The taste is horrible, as if something synthetic has melted on my tongue. I spit and spit into the sink, until the white porcelain is dirtied with yellow stains. Soon all will be revealed – the soulless body, the apple core. Then someone will have to take care of me. I'll no longer be able to pretend everything's okay.

What if literature is both symptom and cure? What if it shifts so imperceptibly between the two that when you believe it to be the one thing, it's actually the other?

Resolution: only read literature that cures the need for literature.

A fat, old fly in the bathroom, buzzing lazily about. I haven't seen flies indoors since I moved to the city from the countryside. There I'd see hundreds of them on the ceiling – they'd have to be vacuumed away. I understand a thousand flies, I understand none, but I don't understand just the one. The sole survivor of winter, perhaps, having spent it hidden away in some ventilation duct?

I lie on the mattress, unable to sleep. I breathe deeply, trying to let thoughts of you slide calmly by. There's one thought, and yet another, and then a third – *let them pass*. Ceaseless, this. I adjust the pillows. I adjust the blanket. How long have I been lying here like this? First half an hour, then an hour, then an hour and a half. I guess that the clock must say 04:30; I look at it. 04:29:44. The minutes and seconds scratch and graze me as they pass, I'm unable to ignore them... Finally I lose count; my muscles relax, the stream of thoughts becomes confused and meaningless – I come to with a start because I can't remember what I was just thinking. The droning hum of some machinery or other soothes me, its frequency so low that I wonder whether it might exist only in my head.

… then, out of the darkness (I've slept, I know that I've finally slept, because it's as if I'm being pulled out of the silence and darkness): a succession of moans from the apartment above. I can actually hear how they're splashing around in each other's DNA, squeezing repulsive juices from their bodies. My mattress is vibrating slightly in time with their rhythm. It continues like this for seven or eight minutes before silence descends. I have to fall asleep all over again. Let thoughts of you pass, adjust the blanket, and so on – but they start up again. I put in a pair of foam ear plugs – it's uncomfortable, the way they expand in there, a kind of crawling sensation, like a couple of insects making their way down each ear canal. With the ear plugs in I can still hear the same noises as before, but now it's as if they've been smothered by a pillow. As I fall back to sleep it feels as if I – or the things inside me that call themselves 'I' – exist somewhere just outside my eyes, or as if my soul has got stuck on its way out of my body.

I don't leave the chair. I live life at a safe distance. I sit here dying as I watch animals die on a screen. The only voice in the room (from morning to night) is David Attenborough's as he tells me about the endangered Amur leopards and the baby elephant, the poor baby elephant that gets separated from its herd and follows its mother's footsteps the wrong way, *straight back into the drought it just came from!*... It's liberating to see just how ruthless and unfair nature is, how certain it is that it's right. Even gazelles are sexually rejected, but they abruptly escape their pain, because something else is in need of food.

I stroked my thumb across your lips and you opened your mouth. I tilted my head towards yours and we kissed. My right hand started a long journey, criss-crossing your body, finally moving down into your underwear, down to the short hairs that tickled until you stopped me. 'This won't work,' you said. You got up, straightened your clothes. I put my forehead against your belly. You held me like that for a while before letting go. You apologised: 'I'm so difficult,' you said, laughing at yourself, surely knowing that this meant something more to me than it did to you and wanting to make it up to me, but there wasn't anything you could do, and I understood, and said that you weren't difficult, believed it too, there and then – at the same time knowing that in a short while, as soon as you no longer stood there before me, as soon as I no longer had your attention, I would mumble the very same words to myself: *You* are *difficult. You're fucking destroying me.* I lay on the sofa through the rest of the night and early hours, watching the sun creep down the mountainside outside the window as I thought about what had just happened, and what should have.

Beauty makes me angry.
Beauty is already a rejection.

A beautiful woman might never make me happy, because what I long for most of all is to be beautiful myself.

I found a piece of meat stuck to my sock just now. I first picked one sock off the floor, then another, and from the second sock fell a small, brownish-red fatty lump, which landed between my feet. But I don't know whether it's food, or something festering and mole-like that's been left to grow in peace in some inaccessible place down there. I inspect both my feet for bleeding sores or craters, but find nothing out of the ordinary. I squeeze the lump and study it closely. Smell it. Pork? No? I don't know. I don't know where it's come from or to what it was attached before the sock. It might have something to do with the cancer, I think, in all seriousness – but only for an instant.

If any of life's surfaces seems convincing I feel compelled to scratch it. Scratch and scratch until something else seeps out. I have squeezed my desire into certain shapes: sentences, typography. Everything so Apollonian and controlled. Now the desire lies pleasingly on the sheets of paper. It lies there in a way that's almost inviting. And so I get the urge to scratch. Until blood trickles out. Until yellow fat and infected, stinking discharge drips down onto your hand, yes, runs down your fingers. Nothing is allowed to be attractive. Nothing is allowed to be static. It's probably an illness I have, some compulsion within me. As I said, I'm not writing to propagate my own misery. I'm fighting the temptation all the time. A temptation that also appears in daily life: I finger the wallpaper and flaking paint, mess up my hair when it sits too neatly, chew my lips until they're left in tatters, and think to pieces every trace of magnanimity I see signs of in myself and others. I get so restless in this room. Everything stands still and I need it to flow.

According to an old notebook I was leafing through the other day, I lost my virginity to Kari on May 4th 2005. The date is handwritten, and all the text says is: '04.05.05. Sex'… There's also a letter from Kari in the book, folded four times. She's drawn flowers around the edge of the notepaper. She writes that she believes in us. I bet I stroked her hair, her eyebrows; looked deep into her big, blue eyes – almost as if I knew what I was doing.

As a child I had the strangest ideas, and would blurt them out at all hours of the day. I would tell my mother my innermost and darkest thoughts, and time and again she would be forced to assure me that it was alright, that no thoughts were forbidden, but it didn't help. Rambling on, even when no one is listening, is the only form of intimacy I understand...

A few weeks ago I woke up completely blind in one eye – I should probably mention this in order to give as clear a medical history as possible. With my left eye I saw clearly on the wall all the light from the streetlamps outside, but my right eye was in total darkness. It took time, perhaps fifteen seconds, before my sight returned – I blinked and blinked, until I saw almost as before.

Every time I'm alone in the apartment and a key is suddenly slid into the lock, it's as if my thoughts are being invaded. Just a second ago they were exactly where they should be, I'd sorted them by rank and formed columns out of them, but now… Someone puts their key in the lock and enters the apartment, throwing off their jacket and shoes? Wanders into the kitchen, for example? Sets groceries out on the kitchen worktop? I get up from the chair and walk over to the door, put my ear against it, try to hear what's happening out there. She's speaking quietly to herself or on the telephone. I hear no individual words, just the tone of her voice. She coughs, sniffles, mumbles on.

Out. I have to get out. On my way down the stairs I see that the door to one of the other apartments is open. I fiddle with the keys to the front door while staring at the open one. A guy on crutches hobbles out from the living room. 'Hello,' he says. 'Hi,' I say. Why am I telling you this? I slip on some wet bloodstains on my way down to the metro, where it always smells of urine. A woman is sitting there, wolfing down peach after peach from a bag, until the bag is empty. I notice I'm wearing odd shoes, one from each of the two pairs I own. One of the shoes is a little too tight, my toes pressing against the inside of the tip. There's a cute, red-haired girl on the ClearChannel advertising screens. A child falls and starts to cry, a howling wail. I feel it in my body, both the fall and the expectation of being picked up, how he simply lies there, helpless. I'm fine-tuned to the pain of others today. There's nothing I don't feel. I don't believe in anything and so cling to everything that makes even the slightest impression on me. I realise that I've already begun to intellectually stagnate.

The sun has disappeared behind clouds long before I reach the water, where biting grey waves are now eating their way up the beach. I take a seat on the only bench, as far from the other man sitting there as possible. Yet another man in a knitted jumper is taking photographs of the sea from various places up on the boardwalk. Out of the corner of my eye I see that he's about to take a photo in my direction, and so I immediately adopt a 'soulful' pose. For some reason or other I think that he's like me. The man on the bench beside me is obviously craning his neck to glance at my notebook, which lies open in my lap. He leans towards me and asks:

'Are you a poet?'

'Not exactly,' I say.

The man sits there for another minute or two, then finally leaves. I peer down at my notebook, which is open to a page on which I have written, in large letters, as the title at the top: 'LONELINESS'…

I blame anything and everything for my loneliness, all the things I don't wish to reveal, but it's precisely the loneliness that I don't want to reveal! (These empty walls.)

The logic of loneliness: *I am lonely, therefore I deserve nothing but to be lonely.*

I'm lonely. What does that thought really mean? What does it imply? It's as if it's become an attitude, something I simply insist on, a point of reference, unlike everything else in life, which simply washes over me like a thick, gooey mass, until it's up my nose and I can't breathe. I insist: *I'm lonely*. Only that. All that is marvellous and chaotic in my life has hardened within this abstraction.

A drunkard came up to me in the park today and asked if I had a lighter. 'Sorry,' I said, and he walked on. I wonder if the people who sit and drink in the parks every day already know each other, or whether their groupings arise organically over the course of an afternoon. Might any respectable man or woman, tired of their usual life, simply sit down among them and tell cock-and-bull stories over cans of beer, and then become one of the gang? The other day, a drunk man with a ponytail and a Hawaiian shirt about to burst said to me: 'Being a good person would suit you.' Now what is that supposed to mean?

All these images, words... but don't we believe in them at the end of the day, the images and words? We believe in them – otherwise we would have given them up long ago. No matter how despondent I might have felt yesterday, no matter how much bitterness I reeled off... the fact that I'm sitting here again today, with my laptop on my lap, means that I do believe. To *write* is to believe, to *love* is to believe – *the inflexible epistemology of obsession*. And somewhere deep within me is an image of us, a blurred vision, a future I carve from the block of stone in my heart. There's no final truth inside it that I can analyse my way towards, or weigh on the same digital bathroom scales I use to weigh my body once a week. There's no ISO standard. The utility of literature and love cannot be quantified or proven, but already exists as an invariable premise for everything else. And my doubt? These dark nights of the soul, alone in bed? It's only the *habit* tempting me: 'Give up,' it says, 'Stand still.'

'Why are you looking at me like that?' You fiddled with your empty glass. You laughed. I laughed. We laughed together all the time back then. We laughed at ourselves. You have no idea of the things your laughter did to me. Your hair fell down around your shoulders, revealing your neck. 'Because...' I couldn't find the words. I laughed. You laughed. At evening's end you said *goodnight* and *goodbye* before kissing me on the mouth. It all happened so fast. Your lips there, and then not there. I kissed you again, and tried kissing you again, but you turned your head away.

'You can't just do that,' I said.

'I'm sorry,' you said.

I burrowed my nose and lips into your hair.

'I'm sorry!' you repeated, but I didn't believe you. Your eyes were wet and shining, but it must have been the streetlights, I didn't believe any of it.

'What do I do now?' I said.

An almost erotic fantasy: that I'm not writing this, but whispering everything into your ear.

It feels good to keep a woman awake all through the night, even if it's only with words!…

Again and again I let language come before thought, before joy, before you and me, and the result is that I run wild on these pages, with passionate nonsense, when what I really need is temperance; so I edit like a madman, censor myself, just as I promised myself I wouldn't, because I'd rather write precisely, coolly, classically; would rather write something that strengthens us both; would rather jump freely from thought to thought, from impression to impression, and, as I've said, from stone to stone, so light on my feet; but this impulse within me to fixate on the worst fucking things, to roll around like a pig in the lowest expressionism, creeps forth all the time – as if *expressing oneself* does any good, as if this thing within me is so brittle and terribly beautiful and breath-taking that I simply can't help myself from showing it off...

I watch an old lady in the park – this will probably be her last spring although she clearly doesn't care. She simply looks at a bird and mimics it: *Ta-tee-ta-tee*... I see children running around, a group of mentally disabled people with their caretakers, dogs on slack leashes, more birds cleaning their feathers in a flowerbed. We're linked together at the roots, I think, far below the ground, like the trees. Even the bird whistling in the tree is connected to the old lady who's mimicking it and both the bird and the old lady are linked to me, watching them both. At least, the world seems to work this way when you're in the right mood. But only very rarely is it possible to *feel* this connection. Maybe only on a late spring day in the park. But it's probably for the best – that it's impossible to feel connected all the time, I mean. I don't know. It's at least a thought it is possible to think; that it's for the best.

Manic laughter is coming from the room next to mine. I'm clearly alone in every way but the way in which I want to be alone. Perhaps it's possible to see the situation in another light? From a new angle? Re-think it, interpret afresh? … Of course! Of course it's possible to look at it differently! In a hundred different ways! A thousand! That's precisely why I've been unable to move on! I've lain stock-still in this gloomy room for hours; have lain in bed and watched the shadows of trees along the walls, how the pointed branches and leaves in the wind make me think of terrified, starving ravens screeching up at the sky. And I've thought and thought. Reached the same conclusion time and again, in an endlessly roundabout way: *I don't want health, I want what I want!* … The laughter increases, and I continue to lie here.

There isn't even a pattern on the ceiling I can study or project myself into. Only white. Only coving where ceiling meets wall, and a cable alongside it. A cobweb in one of the corners. When the rhythm of my heart quickens, when I lose control of my breathing and my breath makes whirlwinds, and these winds capture my thoughts and hurl them out of me, hither and thither about the room, and I no longer know up from down, or right from left, or good from evil, or good from bad, or hatred from love, or anxiety from desire – then the ceiling stares back down at me, with crushing indifference. I try to follow my breath, to not fight it but rather let it wash over me, as I've read in books that one is supposed to do. It seems to work. It's about to work. It has to work.

One's thoughts become clear only upon finding the metaphor that encapsulates the object of one's desire with the least possible ambiguity: a diamond-like phrase, a steady bridge from impulse to action. What we call 'literature' is simply the *waste product of this process*. I have written and written, and come no closer. But *literature* I have no doubt produced: a sage-like sentence here, a stupid one there, a few witty ones, a whole lot of whinging and whining from beginning to end. It oozes and seethes with bodily fluids, with snot and blood and even worse, these things that flow between people. The book has become like a pot full of them, and I've also shoved you (an innocent) into the soup. All so I could find something that I – strictly speaking – haven't found! All the same, I'm in good spirits, because it takes time to make a meaningful life, after all, and love isn't granted to everyone. But I have achieved *something*: something that can be printed and bound, stacked on pallets, wrapped in plastic and sent to bookshops and libraries; be purchased or borrowed, given as a gift, carried around in handbags and backpacks, enjoyed in bed, on the bus or on the toilet (preferably there), and so on.

I have neither the permanence of the rocky shoreline nor the endurance of water, but am like the late winter ice when it melts and then freezes, melts and then freezes. I've never understood principle, or people who manage to go to bed and get up at the same time every day. Good habits have happened to me for certain periods before coming to an end by themselves, but I've never taken credit for any of them. God knows I've tried. God knows I've made battle plans, formulated strategies, imagined myself to be in control. God knows I've sworn never to speak to you again. I melt and freeze over, melt and freeze over. Call it pessimism if you like, or fatalism, but the truth is that I believe in The Good. I believe in improvement and progress. I believe in humankind. I believe in the ice that melts and the water that evaporates, and that everything that must happen will happen, and that one day we'll look back on all this and... well, not laugh, not *that* exactly, but at least sigh resignedly, shake our heads, and give each other a dry, aged peck on the cheek, and die at just the right moment, with everything in perspective, and that our waste will be shaped into ever-changing forms that luckily don't concern us.

A strange new smell has spread about the room – or perhaps I'm only just noticing it now? It's the smell of my own depression, accumulated over several months. Not just semen and sweat as before, not just wet towels, not just pancakes, but all this and more in an entirely new cocktail. The air seems to have taken on some of the qualities of my thoughts: it presses down upon me, insisting on its own importance, then vanishes just as quickly, as if it were never here to begin with. I notice it most when I've been out of the room for a while and then come back in, but immediately get used to it again. It manifests itself sporadically over the course of an evening (at least I haven't been able to identify any pattern). If I'm alert enough, I open the window, but mostly it just hangs there like a fog around me, without me being able to put my finger on exactly what's wrong.

I'm afraid that there's something essentially wrong with me, something deep and unchangeable, which at some point in the future will rise to the surface and destroy everything. Every moment I'm in danger of doing something terrible, something that will forever shut me off from humanity… and what will I do then? What will I do? If one day I act on my contempt – what then? What if I lose my inhibitions? Maybe I've already lost my mind. Maybe I'm not writing this, but standing in the middle of the park, screaming it out loud.

When I was ten or eleven years old I hit a girl in my class for almost no reason at all. Exactly how it happened I don't remember, but I was about to tell her something and she turned away. I don't think she was being rude, she'd simply not heard – but it felt like she was rejecting me. Before I knew what was happening, my hand was rushing towards her head, hitting her temple with a dull thud. I fled the scene straight away and so didn't see her immediate reaction, but I clearly remember her face, the way it always was: how she smiled so kindly, with her big, dumb cheeks. We'd been boyfriend and girlfriend, to the extent that anyone can be said to be boyfriend and girlfriend in primary school. I'd broken up with her. She'd cried then, and I guess I made her cry again.

The blinds are falling to pieces. The cord has got tangled in the mechanism at the top, so you have to pull it hard to open them. The slats are also bent to one side so they never quite close, leaving small gaps looking out towards the window and beyond. They aren't big enough for anyone to see in, just enough for me to see out, but on some days that's bad enough.

Summer is approaching, the trees have turned green. There's no joy in the park now; the birds cry more than they sing. They're not doing so well either these days – they're also horny, wanting more. Flocks of fit, muscled men have started to occupy the area. They pass an American football back and forth and speak in loud voices. Everywhere I see the naked backs of women, both light skinned and dark. Thighs. Calves. Grass between toes. One strokes her hair away from her neck to rub sunscreen on her skin. The noise of sex is everywhere and it isn't morality that prevents me from joining them – I see only emptiness in these strangers. I consider them mirages, or advanced coin-op machines, or scavengers sniffing unconsciously around the park on the hunt for something to feed on. They are nothing but holograms, emanations of some unknown will. None of them wish me well.

In summer, on warm days when sweating, Kari gave off a sweet sort of smell. It wasn't completely lacking in sharpness, but it was still an agreeable smell – it aroused me more than anything else about her. Above all else this smell intoxicates me every time I think back. I associate it with doubt and desire – with the desire she awoke in me and with the doubt that has always accompanied my desire. I associate it with my resistance, my loathing at having to be pulled out of myself towards something other and strange.

I stood washing my hands in the bathroom this morning and studied my eyes in the mirror. As I stared at myself, my face changed around the eyes. In my features I suddenly saw glimpses of my brother – everyone always says I look like him but I'm usually unable to see the resemblance – and I saw my father and mother, my cousins and grandparents. Without changing my expression, my features slipped from hard to soft and then back again; they were repulsive, attractive, strange. I forced a smile and grimaced a few times to make it stop. I dried my hands and went back into my room.

A new woman lies naked in my bed. She has brown eyes, unlike some, and the reddest lips I've ever seen. She squints up at my face to see whether any of the colour has rubbed off on me. I want it to have rubbed off. I refuse to let her scrub it away. I smile. 'Are you a happy person?' she asks. I tell her that I have many joys in my life.

Lately, I've been toying with an idea, a *what if*, a rough draft of a morality, because I bumped into you on the street the other day and felt nothing. It had turned cold again outside; you were wearing a red coat and your cheeks were almost just as red. You smiled when you saw me, stopped, and still I felt nothing. I understood then that the only thing I can be sure of, in the midst of all this, is that no matter what happens the emotion will be a completely different one tomorrow; indifference will turn back into love, love will turn to doubt, doubt will turn to absolute certainty, absolute certainty will turn to inexpressible anxiety, and so on, and that's perfectly fine! It seems I must commit myself to impermanent things, to *impermanence itself*. Because it seems that the meaning of life is to jump to conclusions. To build philosophies using superglue. To say *I love you*, without any kind of backing in the Platonic world of ideas.

I understood all this, and then immediately forgot it.